D1084735

**A love
letter in
illustrated
poetry**

**By
Michael
Hall**

U&I

Michael Hall, the author of the New York Times bestseller, *My Heart Is Like a Zoo*

Published by
Mango Publishing Group,
a division of Mango
Media Inc.

Cover & Layout Design:
Michael Hall

For permission requests,
please contact
the publisher at:

Mango Publishing Group
2850 S Douglas Road,
2nd Floor Coral Gables,
FL 33134 USA

info@mango.bz

Printed in the United
States of America

Mango is an active
supporter of authors'
rights to free speech and
artistic expression in
their books.

The purpose of copyright
is to encourage authors
to produce exceptional
works that enrich
our culture and our
open society.

Uploading or distributing
photos, scans or any
content from this book
without prior permission
is theft of the author's
intellectual property.
Please honor the
author's work as you
would your own.

Thank you in advance
for respecting our
author's rights.

For special orders, quantity
sales, course adoptions and
corporate sales, please email
the publisher at

sales@mango.bz.

For trade and wholesale
sales, please contact Ingram
Publisher Services at

customer.service @
ingramcontent.com or
+1.800.509.4887.

u&i: A Love Letter
in Illustrated Poetry

Library of Congress
Cataloging-in-Publication
number: 2019931490

ISBN:
(print) 978-1-63353-941-9,
(ebook) 978-1-63353-942-6

BISAC category code:
##########

Michael Hall

A love letter in illustrated poetry

Mango Publishing
CORAL GABLES

i remember when i met u.

how i was attracted to u from the beginning.

u'r irresistible smile,

u'r curly hair,

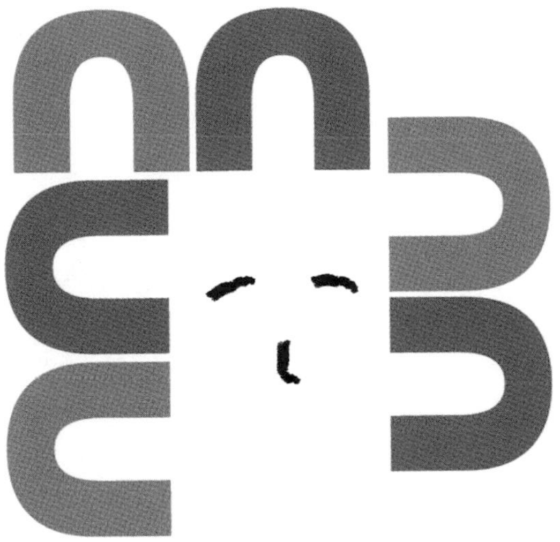

and so on.

u and i went to the theater,

spent an afternoon at the zoo,

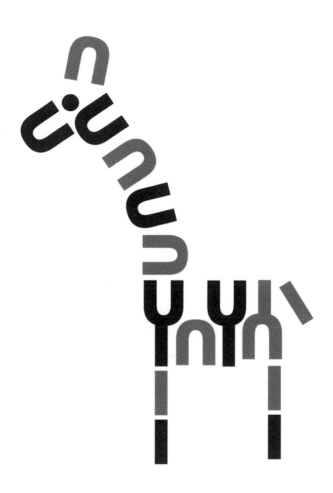

and took long walks on the beach.

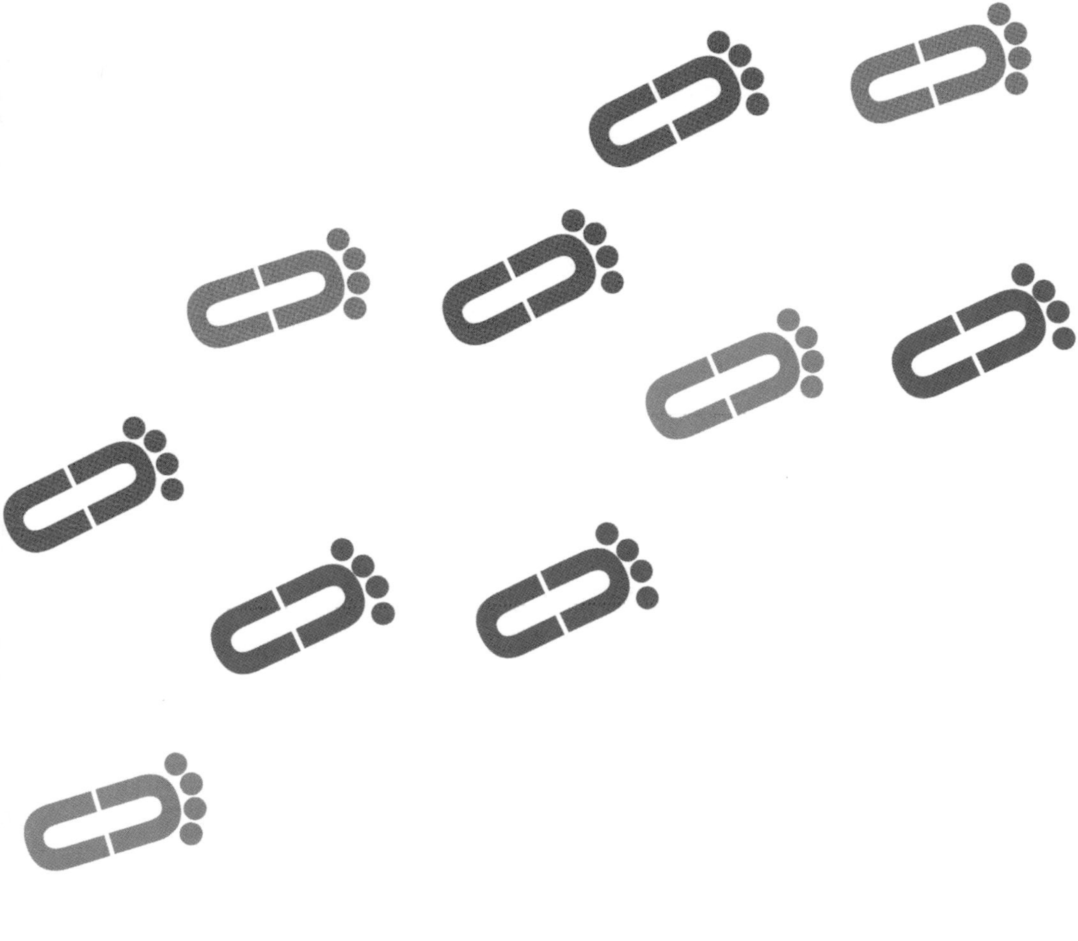

u and i exchanged gifts.

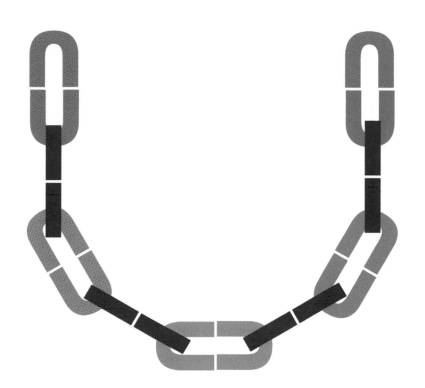

in formal attire, u and i danced at a charity ball

ui

and waded in a fountain in the middle of the night.

u and i became intimate.

when i asked for u'r hand, and you said yes,

i couldn't contain my joy.

i could imagine our lives together:

u and i would sail away,

explore mysterious relics in the south pacific,

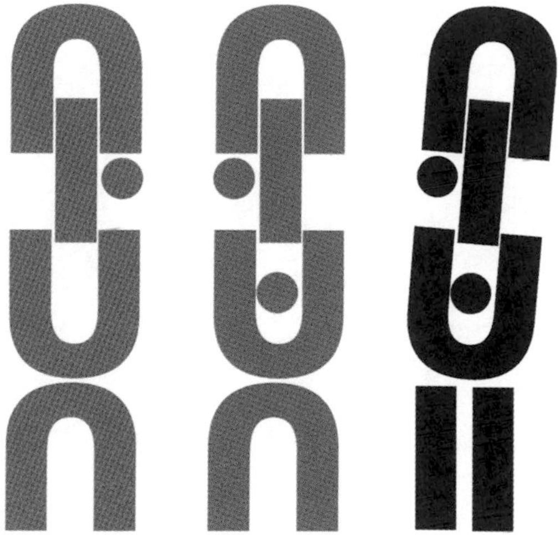

visit spectacular waterfalls,

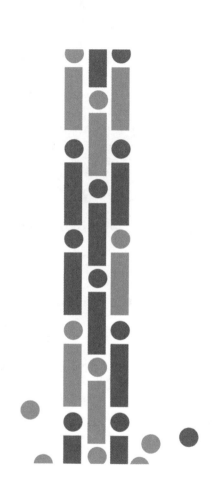

and swim with exotic fish.

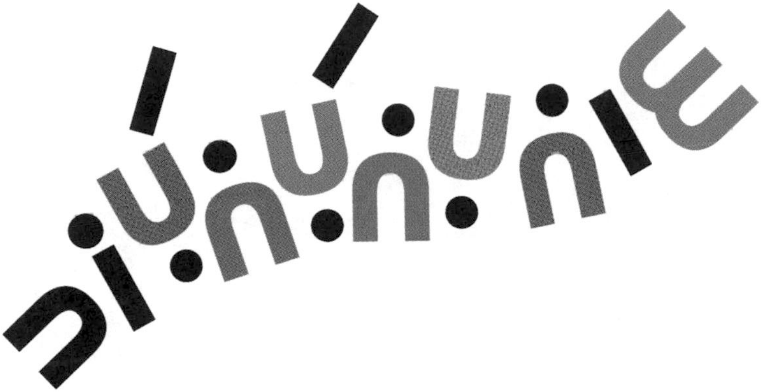

u and i would return to a cozy apartment in the city.

u and i conceive a child.

before long, u and i have a little one.

a few years later, number two comes along.

2

u and i would buy a house in the country

with wild critters traipsing by,

and room for croquet.

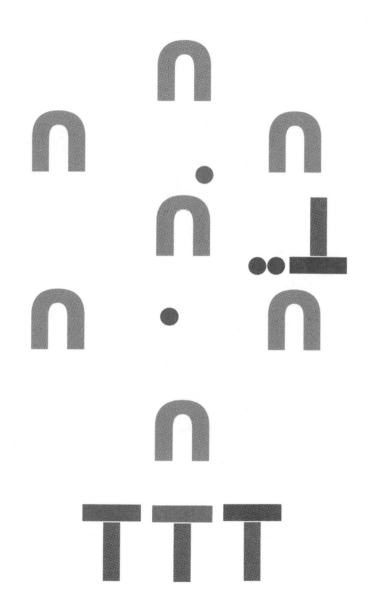

over the years, u and i would watch the children grow.

12

11

things didn't quite work out as i imagined.

u and i weathered some difficult times.

it was hard to juggle all that u and i had taken on.

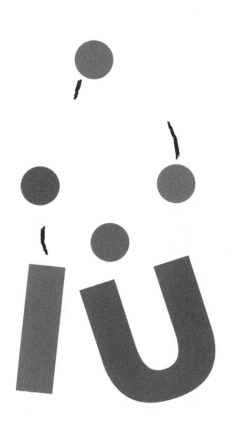

there were money issues.

iou

our differences became sources of conflict.

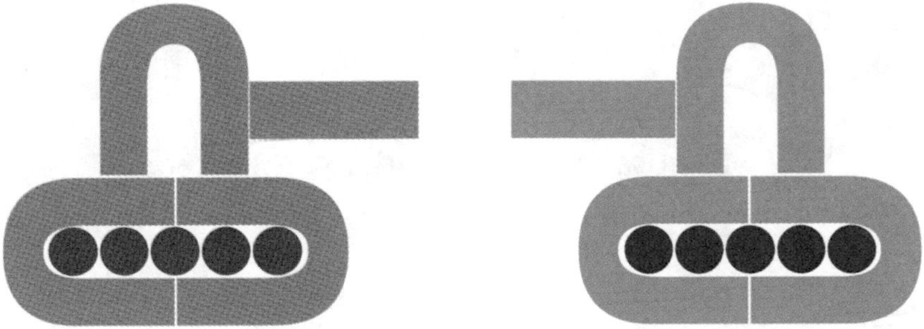

i was absent minded and disorganized.

u kept u'r ducks in a row.

i was prickly.

u were stubborn.

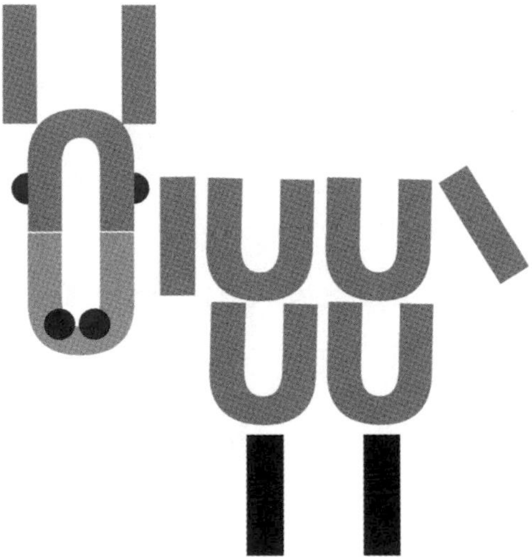

u always seemed to be busy,

while i, admittedly, was prone to idlenss.

i lost my head and said some hurtful things.

u could be pretty fierce, too.

every argument ended in a stalemate.

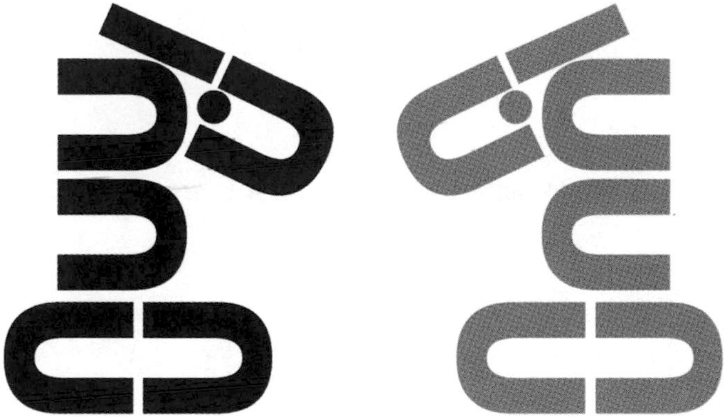

a marriage can feel confining.

sometimes i dreamed of the simplicity of being single . . .

but i no longer do.

over time, u and i locked horns less often

and supported each other more.

u and i found harmony in what was once contentious.

now our lives are woven together like a warm scarf.

years of shared smiles,

and years of shared tears,

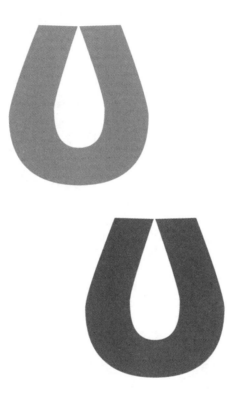

connect us like a sturdy bridge.

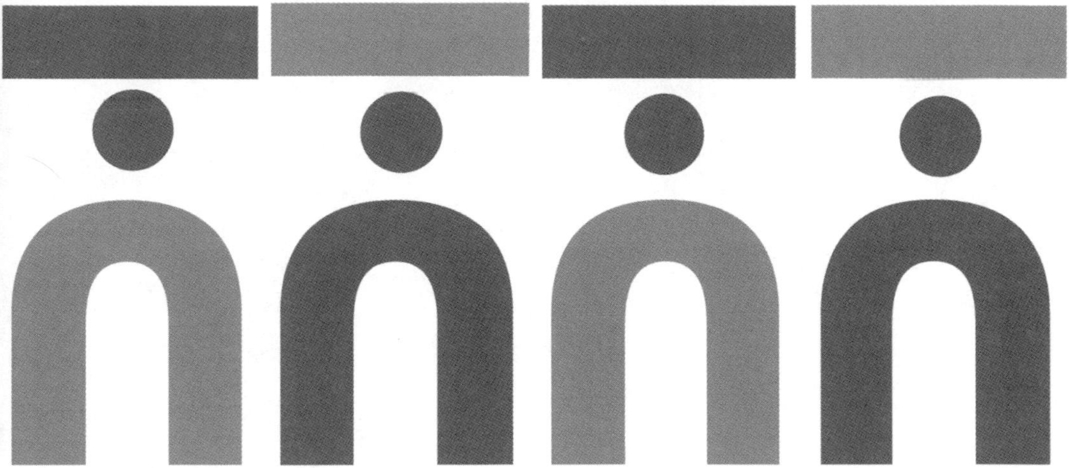

and still, each day, i fall for you all over again.

u'r fire,

u'r grace,

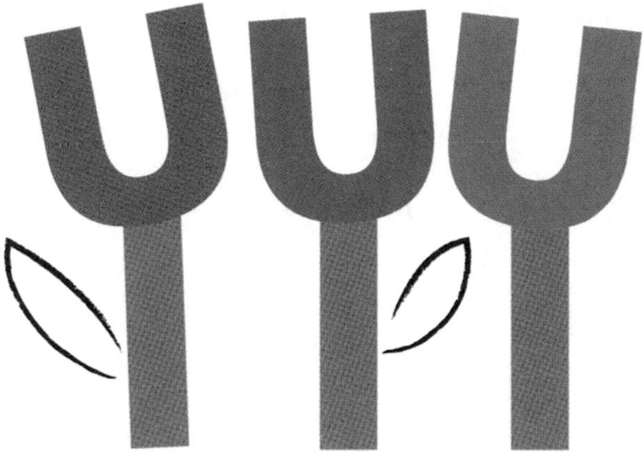

and so on.

for debra

Michael Hall is the author
and illustrator of the
New York Times bestseller
My Heart Is Like a Zoo,
as well as the
critically acclaimed
Perfect Square,
It's an Orange Aardvark,
Red: A Crayon's Story,
and Frankencrayon.